DIMENTIA

RUSSELL COY

CL◢SH

For Olivia

CHAPTER ONE

Chris's arm ripples with unease as he holds it over the open trash bin. It's as though the notebooks in his hand are signaling to him, begging not to be let go.

He allows himself a moment's hesitation then releases his grip on the spiral-bound pads. They make a soft shuffle as they hit the top bag.

Chris lifts a pack of Gold Coasts from the pocket of his sleep pants and wanders from the front corner of the garage to the ratty lawn chair next to the laundry room entrance. He notes the ribbons of dusty afternoon light beaming through the garage door windows.

Chris sighs, exhaled smoke burning his nostrils. He feels like he can sense the notebooks wanting out of the trash.

He can't figure why his mind is kicking up such a fuss. The books are only an offshoot of what he's really throwing away, after all. He pulled the main plug earlier, going through the MS Word folder on his laptop and deleting eight years' worth of short stories and attempted novels.

If pleasure had remained in the act of writing, Chris might have chosen to keep at it. But, the life he's settled into has made writing for fun next to impossible. Monday through Thursday, he comes home with his brain thick and congealed from restoring old brickwork in downtown Indy. Saturdays and Sundays are no better; it's nice having the weekends with Chelsea and Tara, but in a small ranch house like theirs, the noise keeps his ability to concentrate out of reach. That leaves Fridays, and Chris has found little joy in spending those mornings and afternoons re-teaching himself how to write, knowing he'll just lose it again over the course of the coming week. So, he's decided to give up the grind.

Something in the corner of his eye breaks Chris from his reverie. He turns his head toward the garage door and jumps, seeing a backlit shape through the window.

An invisible drawstring pulls Chris's shoulders tight. He can feel the clot of darkness staring back at him. Quick as an arrow, it darts across the row of glass and out of the frame. Chris jerks and drops his cigarette into his lap.

"Shit!"

He leaps out of the chair and slaps at the fabric over his thighs.

Satisfied he's not on fire, he gazes out the window again and finds it empty.

The walls seem paper thin to Chris. A paranoid image jumps into his head of a rotund man bursting through the garage door, swinging a bloody ax.

He remembers Tara right then. Her bus will pull into the neighborhood soon. Chris grabs his cell from his pocket and checks the time: almost three-thirty. Tara makes the walk from the street corner to the front door by herself on most days. Some cowardly part of Chris wants to stick to this routine now, stay inside and hope she'll be fine. He's fairly certain the mystery shadow was just in his head, some weird product of a cloud or trick of the light.

But, the slimmest chance there's someone out there, prowling around for whatever reason, means Chris had damn well better go out there to collect his daughter. He walks to the garage door and pushes the 'up' button on the side wall. The door rising, he looks around for something to defend himself—and Tara, of course—just in case, grabs a snow shovel leaning just inside the entrance and holds it like a baseball bat as he ventures outside.

The sharp November breeze coaxes a raw shiver from Chris as he walks down the driveway. He inspects the row of leaf-scattered front yards to the right which point toward a tight cul-de-sac at the end of Kissell Road. No shadow man. He looks left, where the end of the street offers glimpses of afternoon traffic on Ford Avenue. No shadow man, but a school bus is pulling into the neighborhood.

It halts at the corner, brakes hissing. Tara climbs down off the bottom step, weighted down by her Paw Patrol backpack. The bus takes off toward the dead end, passing Chris. As Tara mounts the curb and sidles up onto the sidewalk, she raises her hand high in the air and waves.

Chris waves back and smiles, putting his Dad face on, which is when he sees the naked man across the street, emerging from behind a tree.

He looks upon the nude form with an odd disconnect as it walks to the road, steps off the curb, and starts across the pavement. His mind adjusts by slow steps, until reality sinks in—this is not a man.

Chris's eyes take in the narrow, goat-like legs teetering under the weight of a pot-belly and breasts hanging down in a floppy W. The skin clothing them is a glossy mixture of dark red with bits of white here and there, like exposed muscle and tendon. Above the creature's thick neck are obsidian slits for eyes and a lower jaw that protrudes outward, displaying long, jagged fangs growing upward like pigeon spikes on a fence.

"Daddy, why are you holding a shovel?" Tara calls, pointing at Chris's hand.

Her words don't sink in. The horror of the creature heading toward the sidewalk takes up all the space in his brain.

A spot of clarity appears as Chris sees the creature's path of travel. It's on a streamlined course toward Tara, watching her intently as a line of pus-like drool falls from its mouth.

"Tara, run to the garage and go inside. Right now," Chris says, trying to keep his voice calm.

As he speaks, he feels his feet treading ground. They're taking him backwards, toward the garage.

What the hell are you doing? his mind yells. *Rush the fucker before it gets to her! Lop its head off with the shovel!*

He continues to recoil, his flight instinct overriding all others.

"What for?" Tara responds.

"What did I just tell you? Run! Get the fuck away from him!"

Tara, nearly to the driveway, furrows her brow, halts, and turns around.

The creature is only steps away.

OHJESUSGODNO.

4

Tara stands unmoving, facing the monster. Chris imagines she's frozen in terror just like him. It reaches for the top of her head with a clefted paw, seems to close it around her hair, and yanks its arm away with a sudden jerk.

Chris stumbles back and falls, ass hitting pavement. A feral *No!* rises to the bottom of his throat and he opens his mouth wide to let it out, but it won't come. A flash like a dying light bulb rises and dies inside him.

He gazes at his daughter's body and wonders dully why she hasn't fallen limp to the ground.

The red abomination reaches out again. Its sharp talons pass through her as though through a hologram, cutting through her midsection without doing any harm. It stops and looks up, casting a sour glance at Chris, then begins to flicker like an old TV on the fritz. Its body loses definition, blinking in and out of reality, then vanishes completely.

"Daddy? Daddy, are you okay?"

Hearing his daughter's voice, Chris realizes she's standing over him. Seeing the fear and confusion on her face, it dawns on him what he must look like, lying shocked on the ground. He wills his composure back to the surface.

"Oh. Uh, yeah, I'm okay. See? Just took a tumble." He forces a goofy expression to his face. "Funny, huh?"

To his partial relief, her expression softens.

"You okay, hon?" says a voice from the road.

The school bus has turned itself around in the cul-de-sac and driven toward them again. The stocky redhead in the driver's seat has her window down and head out.

"Yep, fine," Chris replies. "Just need to re-tie these shoelaces."

He lets out a nervous chuckle. The bus driver nods and drives off.

Chris suddenly feels like passing out, but fights it off and forces himself to his feet.

He looks down at Tara and puts his hand on her back, guiding her toward the garage. "How about Chinese for supper tonight?"

As he says it, he looks over his shoulder, trying to figure out what the hell just happened.

CHAPTER TWO

Tara raises a spoonful of cottage cheese off her plate and turns the spoon sideways, letting it spill back on the dish. Chris chews on a piece of garlic shrimp from the mountain of buffet food before him, watching Tara, but saying nothing to dissuade her. Right now, he'd let her rub the stuff in her hair if she wanted to.

Bubbles of thought float through his head, most of them shots from the scene in the driveway. Chris has come to the only conclusion which makes any sense—that, however real it seemed, the red, fanged creature—

Heh. I dub thee Red Fang!

—had to have been in his head.

The thought brings added questions instead of comfort, and the few possible answers contain words in them Chris doesn't want to consider.

Words like 'tumor' and 'schizophrenia'.

The memory that bothers him most is of his own cowardice, the way his legs took him backward as Red Fang advanced, protecting himself instead of charging toward the beast as it descended on Tara. Chris feels like he's discovered something ugly and unforgivable about himself as a parent.

"Daddy?" says Tara, chewing on a green bean.

Chris straightens in his chair. "Yeah, Princess?"

"When's Mommy coming home?"

Chris shrugs, secretly grateful for the change of subject.

"She'll be back when you get home from school on Monday."

He sticks his fork in another piece of shrimp and stirs it around on the plate instead of eating it.

"'Till then, you got me as your partner in crime this weekend. It'll be fun. Tonight, we can watch anything you want on Netflix, read some more about Alexander Wolf. And then tomorrow, we're going to"—he leans forward for dramatic effect—"the Children's Museum."

Tara's expression doesn't brighten.

"Why'd she have to go away at all?"

Chris holds back a groan. *Tara Albarn, mama's girl to the core.*

"Remember how we talked about it? You, me, and Mommy? Your Great Uncle Keith is really sick. And you know how I had Grampa and Grandma when I was growing up, the way you have me and Mommy?"

Tara nods.

"Mommy didn't have a mommy and daddy, so she lived with Great Uncle Keith instead. And, now that he's sick, she's going to visit him for a little bit."

"Is he going to die?"

Fucking hell. Chris chews the inside of his cheek, considering his response.

"Yeah, hon, he is. So, when Mommy gets back, we have to be really super nice to her."

He raises his eyebrows and holds up a thumb.

"Deal?"

Tara nods and sticks her own thumb up, then goes back to eating.

Over at another table, two older women talk loudly in Spanish. The pudgy, weary-looking one gasps with shocked laughter, making Chris look up and over at them. He guesses the skinny one with thick-lensed glasses just told her something outrageous. Something her old man wanted to try out in the bedroom, he speculates.

Something behind the women catches his eye. Back in the buffet section, on an empty expanse of brick-colored tile, a pocket of blurred space hovers in the air.

What the hell?

Chris narrows his eyes to bring the phenomenon into focus. The rift flickers like heat lightning, stirring up a seasick feeling in Chris's guts.

Cloudy ribbons of phosphorescent green appear and swirl around, taking on mass and detail. Slowly, they solidify into a body and head.

Chris looks, mouth agape, upon a nude round woman now occupying the floor.

Her skin is the color and texture of tree moss. One knee on the floor, arms extended and palms turned up, she curls her long, clawed fingers in a beckoning gesture at the empty air in front of her.

A moment later, a smaller pocket of space forms. It develops like the woman did, by shifts and flickers, slowly becoming a concrete shape. Chris once saw a photo on the internet of a shaved black bear. Its exposed flesh was wrinkled and gray, and a thick snout protruded from its head. This is the closest his mind can come to matching this animal with anything of this world. But, unlike the bear, the four-legged mutant has no eyes above its snout, and instead of two pointed ears, there are four.

Chris's brain dips below full operating capacity, struggling with the sheer surreal *wrongness* of the duo. The rest of the world around him takes on a fluid, underwater quality. There is even a steady, humming pressure in his ears like he's heard while fully underwater in pools and lakes. Chris isn't sure if those things are part of the vision, or of his reaction to it.

Below all that, though, there's another feeling. Something his vision in the driveway didn't have—a feeling of recognition. Unlike Red Fang, he's seen *these* things before, even if he can't say exactly where.

The spectacle continues. The quadruped obeys the green lady's gestures and walks toward her. She reaches out and slides her hand over its leathery scalp and spreads a wide grin. Her hand continues further down the middle of the thing's hide and stops toward its thin tail. She rubs gentle circles around it, then sinks her fingers deep into the quadruped's flesh and pulls out the tail end of its spinal column, as though deboning a fish. The skin comes apart with ease, chunks of gore belching into the air.

The quadruped doesn't seem bothered by this. In fact, the way its forked tongue lolls out, saliva glistening, it seems to make it smile.

The green lady lets go of the vertebral cord, but it stays erect in the air, wiggling as though searching blindly for something. From between her breasts, five fleshy cables emerge and lurch toward the quadruped's backbone. The appendages find and coil around the organ like spaghetti around a fork. They melt into each other, becoming a tube of muscle which elongates and contracts, leech-like, up and down the spine.

The tube moves faster and faster as the moss-toned being tilts her face toward the ceiling. She scrunches her eyes closed and puffs her lips out in depraved ecstasy. A viridescent goo rushes out of the muscle and dribbles down the quivering spinal cord. Her face relaxes and the cylindrical organ morphs back into separate, now-shriveled cables which retract back into her chest. She lowers her head to the quadruped, which tilts its snout upward to meet her. Their tongues fly out and wrap around each other.

By now, Chris has reached a state of shutdown. He stares, blank-headed, as the duo begins to flicker in and out of view. They flutter between *there* and *not there* for several seconds, then pop back into nothingness.

Chris looks around the restaurant. The waitress refills an old man's coffee at one table. The ladies nearby are still laughing together.

"Daddy! Hey, Daddy, hey!"

The finger snap of Tara's voice awakens him. He forces his mind to right itself and puts on a smile that looks more like a grimace.

"Yeah, Princess. What is it?" His voice comes out hoarse.

"I'm done with my plate. Can I have a chocolate sushi?"

This phrase brings Chris back to the rest of his senses. 'Chocolate sushi' is what Tara calls the Little Debbie Swiss cake rolls at the dessert bar against the back wall of the restaurant. He looks that way and lingers a moment on the space where the vision occurred. Everything looks normal now, but Chris still tenses at the thought of approaching the area.

He thinks back to the driveway, to the claw passing

through Tara. If that was all in his head, he reasons, so must the quadruped and its green companion.

"Yeah, hon. I'll go get it for you."

"Can I watch your phone while you're gone?"

Chris rises from his chair and pulls his Android from his pocket, brings up the YouTube Kids app he keeps on his menu for such occasions, and hands the phone over to her.

"Enjoy. I'll be right back."

At the dessert bar, Chris tongs a Swiss roll onto a small plate. The tongs shake in his unsteady hand. He sets the plate down on the tray slide, closes his eyes and breathes, trying to empty his head, then picks the plate back up and turns around.

Heading across the tile toward the carpet, Chris looks across the dining area. At the end of an empty aisle between a line of tables and the booths along the partition, Red Fang stands with its back to the front wall's glass façade.

It stares at Chris, having spotted him first. Its slit eyes and jutted features betray no emotion, but its posture reads as restful.

Chris feels himself start to slip into the same haze as when the two mutants appeared. But this time, he is surprised how easily he is able to keep his mind tethered to reality. He considers the possibility that he's exhausted his capacity for horror, but decides it's more likely from knowing there's nothing really there at all.

Chris makes himself step toward the carpet.

Red Fang steps forward, too.

A grotesque mirror performance ensues. As Chris walks into the dining area, Red Fang matches him step for step. Every heartbeat is a blasting grenade in Chris's chest.

To reassure himself, he recalls a line from *The Shining*: "It's just like pictures in a book, Danny. It isn't real."

With its body language, Red Fang seems to be saying, "Oh, yes I am."

Now, they stand just a few feet apart. Red Fang towers over Chris, who clenches his forearms and shoulders, refusing to let himself shake.

Red Fang stares down at Chris for a moment, then turns its head toward the table where Tara sits watching the phone. A lump forms in Chris's throat. Determined not to falter, he walks over and sits down across from Tara, ignoring Red Fang, even though it has walked over and now stands behind Tara, running its jagged fingers through her head.

"Daddy!"

Tara's tone is insistent. She's reaching out toward the small plate Chris forgot he was holding. He places it on the table and slides it across to her. Tara, ecstatic, picks up the Swiss roll and chomps into it, chunks of cake and cream smearing the corners of her mouth, unaware of Red Fang behind her. Chris picks up his phone, which Tara set down to eat her 'chocolate sushi', and finds a text from Chelsea waiting:

How r things going?

Chris looks up. Red Fang has its arm raised above its head, fingers spread out and wiggling anxiously.

Chris considers his response to Chelsea's text. The responsible thing, it seems, would be to call her and say he's sorry, but something's wrong and she needs to come home right now, that he's seeing things and starting to doubt he can be trusted to care for Tara.

Red Fang swipes at Tara's head, passing through it. This seems to punctuate Chris's line of thinking.

But then, he imagines what would result from telling Chelsea all of that. There'd be tests and scans, a stay in the hospital for observation. Jerry, his boss, wouldn't be sympathetic. He'd lose his job for sure. The bills would start coming. There'd be medications and doctor visits, possibly therapy sessions, none of which he'd be able to afford unemployed.

He weighs his two options—suck it up and get through it, or admit to his problem and start his family down the path to financial ruin?

He types his response to Chelsea:

All good here. How's your uncle?

Red Fang swipes again. Its attempts are measured, with long stretches of time in between. It stares at the back of Tara's head and raises its arm again and focuses.

Chris compromises with himself. He'll arrange a doctor's visit, schedule whatever he needs to on a Friday. In the meantime, he'll grit his teeth and deal with the visions. Now that he knows they're not real, the sharp edges ought to wear down with time. Step by step, he might be able to reach a place where they don't affect him at all.

Red Fang swipes again.

This time, it connects and knocks Tara sideways off her chair.

Her shock draws a bloodcurdling scream from her throat as she hits the floor and rolls onto her stomach. Chris jumps, too, almost tipping his chair backwards. The levelled-out feeling he's slowly regained drops out from under him like a trap door. The urge to get up and flee from the table expands inside him. He puts his hands on the table, intending to push himself up and head back to a safe distance.

Then, remembering his cowardice in the driveway, he stops himself. The urge to retreat is still strong, but Chris gathers all the courage inside him. He bolts to his feet and forces himself to sprint around the table.

Terror makes a jackhammer of his heart as he approaches Red Fang. It's bent over Tara, preparing for another go.

"Hey!" Chris yells.

Red Fang looks toward him and sneers. A noise like the buzzing of a hornet's nest escapes it.

Chris extends his arms and dives at the giant. The last thing he sees is Red Fang spinning toward him, puffing out its saggy chest, and parting its jaw in a mocking hiss.

Their bodies meet. Chris's senses reach maximum volume, and time slows down to let everything in. Red Fang's hide is cold and slick and gives off a sickening odor, like charred bacon and sex. More disturbing, the flesh offers no resistance from the impact of Chris's arms, head, and shoulders. They sink into Red Fang's torso as though it were made of jelly.

The force of his leap carries Chris the rest of the way into Red Fang's body. He emerges into another space—or, rather, a lack of space. There's no blackness, no thudding of the pulse to signify silence.

And then, out of the nothingness, the visions come. They arrive only in glimpses, quick as camera flashes. Chris sees vast walls of jagged stone, their surfaces pulsing like blankets of live rats. Snatches of deformed shrieks piling upon each other flit in and out of Chris's ears.

Just as suddenly, the visions stop. In the void, a tight

crown of sensation forms and widens around the top of Chris's head. It reaches his eyes and he can see the carpet of the restaurant below him. His shoulders, elbows, and legs are born back into his own world. He exits Red Fang's body and lands on the carpet, shaking and disoriented.

Barely thinking straight, Chris rolls over and sees the flaps of excess flesh on Red Fang's back and rump.

Tara, off to the side, looks at him. Her face is wet with tears, and her eyes are wide with trauma and confusion.

Red Fang turns around and looks down at Chris, who feels small as an insect at the monster's feet.

For the first time, it speaks.

"Every time, I am closer."

The buzzing voice makes Chris want to curl into a ball.

"She will feed her soon."

But as the apparitions did moments before, Red Fang flickers and vanishes.

Tara's screams of "Daddy!" take back Chris's attention. She is sitting up now, her palm against her temple, tears streaming down her face.

Chris pushes himself into a sitting position and scoots over. He gathers his daughter into his arms.

"Something hit me, Daddy!"

Chris squeezes her tighter and shushes her softly, trying to calm her and himself down at the same time. He looks around the restaurant and sees everyone pointing their eyes at them.

CHAPTER THREE

"What was it that hit me?"

Tara sniffles and rubs the side of her head in the car seat she's close to outgrown.

Chris registers her question after a moment and wonders the same thing.

A light drizzle has started, filling the deep violet of mid-evening with a stuffy haze. Chris belatedly gives the windshield a single pass with the wipers.

He thinks over how to answer Tara. The truth, which Chris tries to stick to in raising her, seems to be the morally correct choice.

Then, he sounds out the truth in his head:

There's an invisible monster following us around, princess. I thought it wasn't real, but now it looks like it is. I think he wants to get his hands on you to do God-knows-what, and since he managed to pop you one back there, it might not be as impossible as it seems.

Chris wants nothing more than to lie down in complete silence with the lights off.

Instead, he searches for a way to readjust Tara's

mood. He wishes he had a remote control he could click to erase the incident from her memory, delete all the fear and pain. Chris has the same thought whenever she stubs her toe or runs into his and Chelsea's room after a nightmare.

This time, though, it will take more than rocking her in his arms or turning her cries to laughter with a funny voice. He looks at her in the rearview mirror. An idea hits him. He can't erase her memory of being knocked over, but maybe he can change its context.

"Wait a minute," he says. "You mean you didn't see that giant bird in there?"

Tara furrows her brows. "Bird? There wasn't a bird."

"Huh. Well, I guess you wouldn't have seen it, since you were watching my phone when it got in."

Tara stares ahead, considering this new information. Her hand falls away from her temple as her face brightens with interest.

"What kind of bird?"

"I'm not too sure. Big one, though. Both of its wings were as big as our table, I know that. I think it might have been an eagle."

Tara's jaw drops. "An eagle? That's what hit me, really?" She pauses and contemplates the explanation. "How did it get in the restaurant?"

It takes Chris a pause and a bit of thought to work this out.

"You know what, I think it came out those kitchen doors in back, the metal swinging ones back by where the chocolate sushis are, then flew back through them while you were down on the floor. They must have had the back door to the outside open."

Tara considers this, and nods in agreement. "Yeah, I

think that's it. They should keep the door closed from now on."

Chris turns and Kissell Avenue swings into view. "You're right, they should. I'm going to call them when we get inside and tell them to keep all the doors closed now whenever we go there."

"Yeah, so an eagle doesn't get in and hit me."

Despite himself, Chris cracks a genuine smile. "Yep, so an eagle doesn't get in and hit you."

His brief respite flatlines when he pulls into the driveway. In the mist illumined by the headlights, three new creatures loiter in front of the garage door.

The center one stands on six wolf-like legs, an extra pair of fronts in the middle. They hold up a wraith-like torso the color of pus. Its back is straight and rigid, the better to handle what the hairy, orangutan-like forms in front and behind it are doing. At first, it looks to Chris like a bestial parody of double penetration, the rolling-pin girth of two phalluses sliding in and out of the hexapod at both ends. But, as he stares, it becomes clear the behemoths are conjoined by a single organ which skewers the middle mutant like a spit rod through a pig. The way the middle mutant glides back and forth along the flesh-pole suggests it doesn't mind its circumstances.

Chris wonders if they can see *him*. Giving it some thought, he thinks of a way to test this.

He pulls the car forward, riding the break, and honks the horn twice. The copulating threesome takes no notice. The front bumper and engine hood come into contact with the hexapod and the lower regions of the twin apes, all of which dissolve into the area beneath the hood, out of sight. After a moment, the hexapod emerges through the dashboard, as well as the caudal halves of the twins.

The trio now in the car, an ape head floats up to and through Chris. A vision flashes through his mind, just like when he attacked Red Fang. The place is different this time. Chris makes out uneven squares of black and white, along with some pieces of furniture with the same color scheme as rotted teeth.

Contact breaks, and the flashes end.

The monsters drift out the rear of the vehicle and continue mutant-fucking in the rain.

"Daddy, are we going inside or what?"

Inside, Chris puts Tara on the couch, hands her a Capri Sun, and switches on Nick Jr. Sitting on the recliner and rubbing his eyes, he considers the situation.

Everything points to Chris having become some sort of lightning rod for otherworldly phenomena. Tara has already been affected, and it's obvious Red Fang has its eyes on her. Before Chris deals with anything else, he has to get Tara out of harm's way.

He turns toward Tara, leans over, and says, "Listen, peanut, I'm going to my room for a second to call the restaurant about those doors. Don't want that eagle hurting anyone, right?"

"Okay," she mutters, lost in an episode of *Teen Titans Go!*

Chris reflects on the ability of kids to rebound from trauma in the snap of a finger. If only that superpower lasted past age ten.

In the bedroom, he sits on the edge of his and Chelsea's unmade king-size and takes his phone out. He dials, and the click comes on the third ring.

"Yeah?" says a familiar voice, young boys arguing in the background.

"I need you to do me a big favor," Chris says, more forcefully than he means to.

"Hello to you, too, little brother."

"Sorry, long day. Listen, can you take Tara for tonight, maybe the weekend?"

"Say what now?"

"Yes, I know it probably comes as a surprise, but I've got no other choice."

His sister scoffs. "Nice."

Realizing his faux pas, he tries to do damage control. "Look, Bree, you know it's not you or Evan or Joel I have a problem with. It's just that damn trailer park you all live in."

The statement is out of his mouth before he's fully analyzed it. There's a brief silence on the other end of the line.

"You know, divorces tend to be expensive, Chris. Not everyone can afford to live in a house in Fishers."

Chris turns his head back and forth, trying to work some of the tension from his neck. Looking left, he sees what looks to him like a living wire sculpture with a ram's head and the body shape of an ostrich at the far end of the bed, near the tiny flat screen. A fish head on a pair of stumpy legs flicks at the swirling metallic threads with a long stringy tongue, causing them to vibrate. A yellow current passes back and forth between them.

He forces himself to ignore the apparition.

"Instead of me shoving my foot in my mouth all night, can you just agree to take Tara for now? For her sake? When the dust clears, I'll explain everything in full."

"'When the dust clears'? What the hell kind of trouble are you in?"

Chris pauses to think of something sane to tell her. Nothing comes. It's as though his brain has vanished from his skull. He glances at the monsters. Hot, involuntary tears dampen his eyes. He opens his mouth and tries to force something, anything to come out, and at last manages a squeaking, childlike, "Please?"

Bree sighs on the other end of the line. "I'm low on gas, so you'll have to bring her here."

A stray chuckle of relief escapes him. He nods as though she were there in the room.

"Thanks so fucking much, sis. I'll see you in twenty."

He has to sound the words out one at a time, and notices a slur has entered his speech.

CHAPTER FOUR

Emerging into the hallway, Chris halts outside the bedroom door. A steel-blue wraith lies on the carpet. Hovering over it, a dog-sized centipedal body with twin heads on elongated necks inserts mosquito-like proboscises into openings under the wraith's raised arms.

Chris stares, dead-eyed.

A loud thump flies into his ears, followed by Tara screaming in pain. Chris breaks out of his trance, hops over the wraith and centipede, and runs into the living room.

Tara, lying on the hardwood floor, wails and tries to push herself up.

Red Fang, standing over her, extends its arms out like a monster in a 1950's movie poster. It bends down and scoops up Tara from the floor. She lets out a piercing scream as a rictus of terror floods into her face. She falls through Red Fang's grip like flour through a net, hitting the floor again.

Chris runs to his daughter, picks her up, and backs up to a safe distance. He looks Red Fang in its thin, black eyes while trying to keep his breathing slow, his expression rigid.

Red Fang's laughter invades his head like poison smoke.

"I'm close to your world now," it hisses. *"So close I can touch her. I've spent so long down there, building my strength. In your world, we've only just met. In mine, ages have passed since our last visit. But, each time I return, our connection is stronger."*

Chris tightens his hold on Tara.

"What connection? What makes her so special for you?"

"Not with her. With you. You've allowed your link to my world to grow, and I can use it to enter yours, as I've done with so many others. Soon, your daughter will join Mama and me down there. She will feed Mama, like the rest of them."

"You're not touching my girl." He manages a little backbone in his voice. "Get the hell out of my house!"

"I can do what I wish. You exist only to be a portal for me to enter this world, and she exists only to be food for Mama. You don't need to understand or accept anything. Fight all you want, because it will change nothing."

Red Fang flickers out of sight, leaving behind an echo of laughter.

Chris, still carrying Tara, snatches her backpack off the coat rack beside the front door, hurries back into the hallway, and bursts into Tara's bedroom. He sits her on the *Shimmer and Shine* themed sheets covering her mattress and has her roll up her sleeves and pant legs to check the damage from hitting the floor. There's a nasty red splotch across her right knee and a few other welts.

He kisses her on the forehead.

"Listen, peanut," he slurs, "you and me are going over to Aunt Brianna's. She really misses you and wants to play with you, so you're going to stay with her for a little while, okay?"

Tara sniffles and doesn't respond. Chris unzips her book bag, spills her iPad and daily achievement folder on the mattress, and stuffs a couple of random outfits in the bag.

The whole time, he attempts to decipher what Red Fang's words meant.

His mind latches on to one of the last things it said:

"Now you've allowed your link to my world to grow."

What link to what world, Chris wonders, and how has he allowed it to grow?

Once they're back in the car, Chris realizes, in a scattered-puzzle kind of way, what Red Fang might have been referring to.

Chris reaches up to the sun visor and pushes the button on the device clipped to it.

In the glow of the rain and headlights, the garage door opens.

25

CHAPTER FIVE

The splatter of rain outside gives the inside of the garage an eerie, silent feeling.

Chris leads Tara to the trash bin and sets her bookbag down beside him. He lets go of her hand and guides it to his jacket tail.

"You hold onto me, baby, and don't let go, no matter what."

He extends a pinkie toward her. Still shaken and sniffling, she wraps her own around it.

Chris flips the bin open and plunges his arm in, retrieving the notebooks he tossed. Time has made the oldest one frail, so much so Chris half-expects the paper to crumble as he opens to the first page.

He got the first notebook when he was twenty-three, not long after he started writing. He'd come to a grinding halt on his attempt at an old-school crime novel in the vein of Jim Thompson. Looking for any way to get the ideas flowing again, Chris decided to give automatic writing a shot, having read an article on it by an author he admired. He sat at his father's desk, looked away, and started scribbling.

He didn't expect the pungent smell which attacked his nose, nor the flicker in his vision just before blacking out. Coming to, he found several pages of what seemed like random words, no spaces between them.

The ink, somewhat faded, is still readable after all this time. Its first few lines read: *Blackwhitesquarescrooked-bigfootswallowsfriendinrottentoothbenchgreenwoman-fucksmonsterspinetentacleswrappedaround eachotherlittileguyslidesbetweentwojoinedmen*...

Chris recalls the flashes of black and white in the driveway.

(*littleguyslidesbetweentwojoinedmen*)

The part about the green woman fucking a monster leaps out at him.

The images meant nothing to Chris that first time. He put them down as being stray pictures from his subconscious which needed to be flushed out, because after that he was able to write again. It became a semi-regular practice from then until today. When he was stuck, he would grab a pen, tune out, and come out on the other side with pages of stray phrases and descriptions.

He shudders, realizing that all this time, he may have been peering into an actual nether-realm. Red Fang's other statement, about using Chris's link to enter this world and get at Tara, suddenly seems more real and horrifying. His hand travels to Tara's shoulder and pulls her a bit closer.

To what end does Red Fang need her? Chris thinks of the witch in Hansel and Gretel, of the Giant in Jack and the Beanstalk. He can't imagine Red Fang going to such great measures to simply devour his daughter. For a brief and horrible moment, he thinks of what the human monsters in his own world—the abductors and serial killers—usually want children for. To preserve his sanity, Chris shuts down this line of thought.

He shuts off the overhead garage light and leads Tara back through the house and out the front door. The few seconds in the rain soak them as they make their way to his car. Chris buckles her in and jumps in the driver's seat. He starts the car and backs out of the driveway, halting in the road so he can shift into drive.

In front of them, in the glow of the headlights, Red Fang stands, the rain and light surrounding it with a diseased radiance.

Chris brings his hand to the gear stick, throws it into forward, and steps on the gas. He turns the steering wheel sharp to the right.

"Tara, hang on!"

Red Fang drifts into the periphery of Chris's vision as he rides the passenger side on and off the curb. He and Tara bounce in their seats, making Tara shriek.

Not looking back, Chris heads toward the stop sign. His fingers remain flexed and aching around the wheel. The road before them is clear, right up until Red Fang descends into view, landing on the car's hood with a bang.

Chris lets out a quick yelp while mashing the brakes. He feels his insides wrenched around as the car weaves in the slick street. It comes to a near-stop, but Chris's foot slips off the brake pedal when Red Fang explodes through the windshield headfirst and reaches in toward him.

He feels the rough texture of a rain-dripped claw as it grabs him by the throat. Up close, Chris sees Red Fang's flesh suit of muscle and cartilage.

Tara screams. Red Fang reaches between the seats with its free hand. Trapped against the seat by the strength of the grip, Chris looks into the rearview mirror to see the struggle in the back. Just barely, he sees Red Fang gripping his daughter by the hair and lifting her upwards, trying to extract her from the seatbelt's hold like a stubborn tooth. Tara hits, kicks, scratches.

Chris searches for the largest shard of shattered glass he can find. He settles on a sliver the size of a nacho chip and pounds it through the back of the hand restraining him, using his own palm as a mallet. There is pressure, but no pain, as its edge breaks the surface of Chris's skin while penetrating deep into Red Fang's. Black fluid pours from the monster's wound and blood from Chris's body.

Red Fang hisses in pain but doesn't release its grip on Tara. Instead, it tightens its hold on Chris's throat. His lungs fight against the sudden lockdown. The world starts to skip and flicker. He sees nothing like in the notebooks. No diner, no mutants. Only flashes of a dark, damp place, the same place he experienced in the Chinese restaurant.

Red Fang lets go of his throat and the flashes stop. It backs out of the windshield, and to Chris's horror, is taking Tara with him, holding her hair as though gripping a pumpkin by the vine. It lets out an echoing laugh as it spasms between *there* and *not there*.

Tara's flickering, too.

"No!" Chris howls.

He scrambles out of his seat, but they are gone by the time he starts climbing over the steering wheel.

The remaining glass framing the windshield's bottom rakes across Chris's shirt and shorts as he crawls out onto the hood of the car. Ragged, incoherent sounds leave his mouth. He lies stomach down and listens to the sound of rain pounding metal. His hair and clothes grow wetter. The vision in his left eye is gone, replaced by a searing pain in his cornea from a shard of windshield entering his eye.

For the first time, he notices the house he's crashed into. The car was rolling the whole time Chris was fighting Red Fang. It crashed into a section of vinyl siding, just missing a front window.

Red and blue lights appear in the corner of his good eye, the sound of sirens accompanying them.

CHAPTER SIX

"Sir? Sir, are you conscious?" says a woman's voice, thin as a whisper from down a well. There is a pause for response. Chris doesn't give one.

"If you're able to, raise a hand or leg to let me know you can hear me."

Chris plays possum. Maybe she'll go away and leave him to his pain and horror, to the copper taste of blood on his tongue.

"Dispatch, what's our ETA for emergency services?" She speaks in rapid staccato. "Copy that."

A shuffle and jangle. Cautious footsteps.

"Okay, I'm going to approach and check for a pulse."

Realizing she isn't leaving, Chris lifts his own hand at the wrist. The officer lets out a clipped syllable-"Whoa!"

Her footsteps pause.

"Sir? Sir, can you speak?"

Chris finds he cannot.

"Emergency, driver is responsive, but appears to be in shock. Okay, I see you. Sir, an ambulance is on its way. Can you tell me if you're in pain?"

He keeps his silence. Sirens in the distance get louder and closer.

———

In the ambulance, limp on a stretcher, Chris's body registers in his head as something separate, *other*. Sensations pass through it like lumbering clouds: the IV pricking his arm, the sideways shift of gravity when the driver hangs a turn. Latex fingers hold Chris's good eye open while a thin white light burns his pupil.

He tries to sit up. The paramedic on the right puts a hand to his chest and guides him to lay back down.

"Whoa, now, friend," he says. "Just relax for the time being and we'll take care of everything."

The sudden, hot dizziness of sitting up takes any fight out of Chris. He lays back down.

After a while, he is pulled from the ambulance and wheeled on the gurney through automatic doors and under a path of rectangular ceiling tiles and florescent lights. Nurses gather around, slide an oxygen mask on his head, and cut his T-shirt down the middle. His protests come out as mumbles, like talking in one's sleep.

A doctor appears and speaks to the nurses while examining Chris. She pays special attention to the eye Chris can't see out of. A few minutes later, an IV is inserted and he feels himself pulled into a cavernous sleep.

———

Chris resurfaces after midnight, stomach clenching with faint nausea. The familiar, stinging smell of hospital pings in his nose. He strains to adjust his vision to the bright ceiling light, which casts a circular glow around him from above. Shadows loiter past its edges.

He can tell they've given him the real King Kong stuff —morphine. His head feels like it's been filled with wet clay, but the heat and delirium are gone.

He fights to remember how he got here. Flashes of his car and neighborhood surface weakly and sink quick.

Something stirs in the shadows beyond the ceiling light.

Chris squints against his skewed vision. In silhouette, near the opposite wall, an armadillo-like body lays on its back. A translucent blob with flamingo-like legs hovers over it, invaginating the ends of its mouth-ended limbs with thin flagellum. Their rutting produces guttural squeals and high-pitched grunts.

Chris's mind fills with fresh horror and the memory of Tara being snatched from the car returns. Everything comes flooding back, his nausea rising to an acidic peak.

Chris's thoughts race and collide with each other—

Where is she now?

What's being done to her?

Is she even still alive?

He doesn't know where to begin finding answers.

The prospect of Tara being lost forever stretches out before him. He pictures the toys on her bedroom floor piled in cardboard boxes, collecting dust; her school bus passing their street by, one seat emptier.

Hot tears flood Chris's un-bandaged eye. He lowers his head back to the pillow, tempted to give in to the hollow stupor the opiates in his system offer.

The squeals and grunts from across the room grow too loud to block out. Chris rolls his eye toward the mutants and watches them a moment, resigning himself to his new reality.

Something on the wall behind them catches his eye. An oil painting hangs in a white frame, surrounded by matting. The image depicts a lake surrounded by forest and mountains, the sort of generic representation meant to calm the sick and injured. In the foreground of the picture, an eagle flies low above the water, holding a stray branch in its claws.

Chris thinks of the tale about the restaurant eagle he spun for Tara, just a few hours back. He'd built her a shelter from the terror surrounding them, using his imagination.

And that was a slap upside the head and a fall from her chair, a voice in his head chides. *Now, the fucking Bogeyman is carrying her through some mutant hell dimension, and what are you doing? Come on, time to get off your ass and go get her. There'll be plenty of time to sit cozy and high afterward if you make it through alive. No more plopping your ass down in the driveway.*

A quiet ember ignites in Chris's gut. His nostrils flare. He makes a fist with his uninjured hand, nails almost breaking the flesh.

Moving his eye from the painting back to the ceiling, Chris puts his brain hard to work, boiling the situation down to its simplest terms.

All right, Chris, first things first. What's the problem? Simple: my daughter has been stolen into another dimension for purposes unknown.

Goal? Get her back.

Okay, how? Chris doesn't have to think about this for long. *Go into the other dimension myself and find her.*

Fair enough, but how?

He looks again at the lovers in the corner, thinking about the rest of the mutants he's seen through the evening—in particular, the ones in the driveway he rolled his car through.

"Hey, you two!" Chris hollers and claps loudly.

No response. It's as though they're not actually in the room, like their presence is some kind of projection or broadcast. He remembers what Red Fang said in his living room, that it had had to build its strength and its connection to Chris in order to come into this world.

Maybe he can do the same with them. If he lays a hand on one, he knows he'll see into their dimension. There has to be a way he can boost the connection to where he can also enter their world.

Maybe it's a matter of frequency, Chris speculates. Like turning the knob on an old-school radio to make the station come in clearer. He wonders what would happen if he tried adjusting his mind to the mutants' wavelength while touching them.

You won't find out just lying there.

He reaches over the plastic side rail to his right and pulls the release latch, lets the rail down, and removes the blanket from his lower half. Swinging his legs over the side turns the low ache in his body to outright agony. Chris looks around the morphine drip for a self-serve button and finds none.

He accepts that he'll need to pull the needle from his arm. Another issue presents itself: when he removes the attachments keeping track of his vitals, an alarm will go off. Nurses will come running. He works his head around the problem for a minute and comes up with something, but knows he'll have to be fast.

Chris peels the strip of medical tape loose from the IV

and slides the needle out, nice and steady, and then tears a strip of Kleenex from a box on the bed tray, wadding it up and laying it against the puncture wound.

He climbs weakly off the bed and flips up the wheel locks on one side of it, then crawls over the mattress and does the other side. Only the sensor clip and pressure cuff remain now, and there will be zero room for fuck ups here. Chris allows himself a moment to close his eyes, take a few deep breaths, and clear his head.

He rips the finger clip and cuff away from his arm. Distant alarms begin beeping. Gathering all his strength, Chris grabs onto the end of the mobile bed and hauls it over to the open door. The door is heavy and it seems to take forever to swing it shut, long enough for him to catch a glimpse of the scrub-clad bodies rushing out from behind the nurse's station. Finally, the door bangs into the frame and clicks. He rolls the bed up to the door and latches the wheels in place, getting the last one just before the knob starts jiggling. The door opens a crack then gets stuck against the bed.

"Mr. Albarn?" says a male voice, followed by the repeated slapping of a palm against the wood.

Chris ignores it and turns toward the rest of the room. His open-in-the-back gown lets the cold air lick his body as he limps across the linoleum. His heart clangs like a church bell in his eardrums as he approaches the pair of mutants, who still take no notice of him. Reaching the squelching beasts, Chris hesitates and feels his stomach tense and rumble. The rumbling is more severe and acidic than dope nausea. Quaking, he kneels down close, reaches out, and places his palm against the mutant's holographic surface.

Below the blob and armadillo beings, the black-and-white checkered floor of the diner spreads outward, overlying the hospital floor. Chris can still feel the chilly hard linoleum, though, and knows it is still just an illusion.

Ordering himself to go deeper, he tries to sense through his palm what the blob's flesh might feel like. It appears slick and squishy, so he moves his hand along the skin and imagines it as feeling like raw liver.

By slow increments, the touch begins to solidify, the blob developing a repulsive warmth. It jerks away. Chris, startled, yanks his own hand back in response. It felt *him*.

Spurred on, Chris returns his hand to the mutant. It jerks again, but Chris doesn't, even when the blob starts to vibrate and tighten. There is a terrible spasm throughout its body and a yellow, colostrum-like substance seeps out.

Chris doesn't let it derail him—things will probably get grosser than this, based on what he's seen of the diner's other patrons. He soldiers on, letting the sensations he described from the notebooks fill his mind. Odors, textures, and sounds surround him. The smooth stiffness of the hospital floor changes, morphing into a damp pliancy, like rotted wood.

He feels his own world dissipate by slow increments, until there is nothing left of it.

A new environment has taken its place.

He looks up from the blob at his new surroundings, and sees that his experiment has succeeded.

He is now in the world of the mutants, and of Red Fang.

CHAPTER SEVEN

It takes a moment for Chris to absorb the shock. He's gone from standing in the hospital to lying in semi-darkness, no gradual transition. He pushes himself up with his palms, the texture of the floor bringing to mind stacks of soggy paper. On either side of him, slabs protrude at shoulder height from chipped partitions. A rectangle of shadow floats above his head. He scoots forward, emerging feet first into open space filled with dingy half-light.

His eyes drift across the black-and-white diamond pattern of the floor, then to his right where a wall covered in unfamiliar symbols, overlapping like years of graffiti, stands a few feet away. He swings his head the other way and sees rows of diner booths, light gray and pocked with brown craters as though sculpted from rotted teeth, extending to the other side of the room.

Pain gushes through Chris as he stands up. Uncomfortable silence fills the air.

Is Tara here, he wonders, scared and frozen in one of these booths?

He hears a short gurgle behind him. He wrenches his head over his shoulder and stumbles, the suddenness of movement interrupting his balance. He sees nothing behind him, turns back, and begins down the strip of open floor.

Rapid steps behind him, the low gurgle droning beneath it.

Chris halts, paying attention to where the scurrying ends. He turns, gently this time. His eyes land on one of the cavity-marked benches. He inches toward it, body thrumming with adrenaline. Something white and thin whips in and out of view.

Chris's nerve disappears and he starts to back up. He's managed half a step when a mass of long tendrils leaps out from behind the bench and jets forward, its gelatinous body colliding with Chris.

His scalp hits the floor and the inside of his head roars with pain. Tiny claws dig into his chest. Tendrils wriggle and crawl along his arms, legs, torso, and face. He looks up at the mass of dripping ooze perched on his ribs, freezes in the glare of seven protruding eyes. The tendrils find Chris's facial cavities, breaching his nose and attempting to push through his fastened lips.

Chris twists his head to the side and tries to bury his face in his shoulder, then attempts to raise up and cast off his assailant. The free tendrils wrap around his wrists, showing their strength as they tighten and push his arms to the floor, holding him in a crucifixion pose. Needing to breathe, he releases his mouth from his shoulder and gasps. The thin appendages rush in.

Chris feels as though a hundred worms are slithering into his throat. They continue down into his stomach. He shrinks from the pain and violation, closes his good eye.

"You like it?"

The voice is deep and vibrating, like wind in a tunnel.

"I love how you wiggle. You must be enjoying yourself."

The tendrils drive deeper into Chris, stretching his stomach walls, a few passing into his lower organs. He directs his thoughts toward his captor, sending out a screaming message: *"No! No, I don't like it! Please stop!"*

A long, low gurgle sounds from the body on Chris's chest. *"Of course you do. We all like everything here."*

Chris rattles his head side to side. *"I'm not one of you. I just came here to find my daughter. Please, just take me to someone who can help me."*

Chris's spirit has withered, and even the voice in his head sounds weak to him as he pleads.

He opens his good eye and sees the tendrils sweat something black and oily. A harsh taste attacks his tongue. Drops of the fluid fall on his face and chest. He wishes his mind would revert to the blank slate it became after Tara was taken from him, but it refuses. Tears run down the side of his face, mixing with the oily excretion.

At last, the tendrils relax, then slide out of him. His lungs come awake and greedily suck in the air, releasing it in painful coughs.

A wet flagella caresses his face.

"All done, now. You want to talk to somebody? I'll take you, for being so sweet."

Chris shudders at how the voice draws out those last words, then finds the hold on his arms released, the weight on his chest lifted. There is a tug at his still-bound ankles. The floor starts dragging along his back. He looks down and sees the lumbering blob ahead, shuffling a foot at a time, jerking Chris along in short heaves.

He feels pain, disgust, and humiliation, real as the black fluid that spilled on his face. A hot rage forms, sizzles, and explodes. He tries to lunge upward, intending to grab the tendrils holding his feet, drag the gelatinous form to him, and splatter the room with shreds of it.

Instead, he flops limply before returning to the floor, exhaustion overcoming his fury.

There is a sharp turn, then another. The mass of tendrils dives below Chris's line of vision. He raises his head and sees it descend into an opening in the floor. His own body follows, vanishing into shadow. The surface under him turns rough, scraping his heels.

Chris feels himself on a steep, curving, downward incline. His hands brush against close-together walls. His scalp knocks against the floor, making him draw a sharp breath between his gritted teeth. He lifts his head and keeps it elevated to prevent more damage.

The floor flattens out as they emerge into open space. A low ceiling of uneven stone, splattered with brown mold, meets Chris's eyes. He tilts his head up to observe his new surroundings. His mouth drops open.

The space is so vast there seems to be no opposite end, and filling it is a sea of impossible lifeforms.

The tendrils around his feet drag him into the gathering. They pass a hairy behemoth with rat teeth and eyes in the double digits. It opens its mouth wide and lowers it onto the head and body of a man-sized reptile with spikes growing down its back, engulfing it like a snake ingesting a horse. Immediately, the giant loses its hair in large clumps, going bald in seconds. Its pale flesh turns green and scaly. Its jagged fangs fall out and land in a pile of other discarded teeth. Its body elongates and thins out, head reshaping into a replica of its amphibian friend.

Fully transformed, it coughs up a phlegmy ball of hair which falls and rolls a few feet across the goo-covered floor. Something seems to poke and shift within the caul. Limbs sprout from it. The hair grows thicker, now covering a full body. A pair of rat fangs break through the gums. What was once a compact mass is now the spitting image of the behemoth prior to its transformation. It turns toward its partner and opens its mouth wide, starting the cycle all over again. The whole incident happens within the space of a few seconds.

Pulled deeper into the throng, Chris catches glimpses of misshapen heads with too many eyes. There are wet sounds and hisses. The stench of the place reaches into his mouth and nose, invasive and horrible as the jumble of flagellum had been.

Chris slides past the hexapod from earlier in his driveway, still hunkered on all sixes and sliding along the meaty shaft conjoining the fat twins. The other visions he had back in his own world are also made flesh here, alongside countless new horrors.

The movement stops. Chris feels the tendrils unwrap from his legs. He takes a moment to move his tingling feet around, let the blood flow back in. By now, his desire to rip apart the creature that violated him has passed. Some of the strength has returned to his body, but his will to fight is sapped. The overload of unnatural sights has made his brain scattered and dull.

He registers the sudden shift in the cavern. The noise dies down to silence as though a plug has been pulled. In the sudden quiet, Chris hears bodies scuffing along the floor, feels a galaxy of eyes turning toward him.

Squelching footsteps a distance away.

Chris reluctantly raises his head and points his eyes to their source.

In the middle of the gathering sits a platform of flat brownish rock with a jagged throne carved into its center. Walking from the throne to the edge of the platform is the clawed, green woman Chris saw in the Chinese restaurant. Her eyeless, four-legged companion stays back at the throne, standing at attention.

She holds her short, chubby arm out to the creature that brought Chris here, who stands a respectful distance from the platform. It reaches a single tendril out and touches its tip to the mossy open palm in front of it. Its seven eyes are closed, as are the green lady's.

Remembering the wordless exchange in the diner, Chris guesses they are communicating. About him, obviously. A creeping dread falls on him as he wonders what lies in his near future.

Is he being referred to in the conversation as a guest? As a potential slave to be used for the pleasure of this crowd? As dinner?

The green lady drops her hand back to her side and opens her eyes, directing them toward Chris, as his seven-eyed attacker moves away from the platform and joins the others. Chris finds enough energy to sit himself up, fore-arms holding him aloft. He raises his knees in preparation to jump. The green lady extends her arm and motions for him to approach.

Chris leaps awkwardly to his feet, turns around, and stumbles toward the crowd. His muddled plan is to plow through them and crawl back up the spiral stone chute. There might be an exit up there.

He hears the pounding of paws on the cavern floor, along with gales of rapid panting. They don't reach his ears in time for him to prepare for the appearance of the green lady's eyeless companion, skidding to a stop in front of him. The collision sends him to the floor on the other side of the canine. His system seizes from the shock of the fall, lungs and heart struggling a moment before starting again.

A warm wall of fur nudges the side of Chris's face. A paw, thick as his own hand, grabs his shoulder and pulls him onto his side. Confusion turns to panic as what looks like a thick whip made of segments of bone lashes around his throat. It hoists him up by the head so that he dangles at the canine's side.

The familiar roughness of being hauled across the ragged floor ends with the edge of the stone platform dragging along his hip and legs like a dull knife. The canine releases him from its spinal grip. The back of his head lands on something cushiony and wide.

The green lady's upside-down face comes into view above him. Chris trembles as her eyes—dark amber bulbs with a long pupil slicing through the middle—descend and engulf his vision. His stomach clenches at the smell falling from her.

"Does the little mouse like being chased?"

The voice is a steamy hiss between his ears.

"We're glad you found your way here, little mouse. There are many of us who love to use our claws."

Jagged fingernails drag along Chris's arm. He focuses on emptying his mind of the terrible things which will probably be done to him. He closes his eye and sends out a thought, hoping the green lady receives it.

"Please don't hurt me. I'm not here to play any games or be a part of whatever goes on here."

He hears a low gurgle.

Is she laughing?

"Of course I am, you sneaky mouse. It always amuses me when a new one pretends to beg. Plus, your nickname for me is hilarious. 'Green lady'. If you can't think of anything more creative, just call me by my true name—Banguai. Also, you don't have to pretend with me. Your sort of pleasure isn't to my taste. But, don't you worry—we'll find you a suitable playmate."

Now, Chris understands he doesn't need to focus to send his thoughts to her. Instead, he'll have to be careful what he allows his mind to produce at all.

"I swear I'm not pretending, Banguai. Listen, I'm not from here. I crossed over into this world from another place."

"We know that, dear. All of us have, also. One grows so tired of the lack of options there. The same wilting phallus, the same few apertures. In this place, you can take whatever form is your true self at the moment. Grow and discard pleasure organs at will. You can go eons without having the same sensation twice, if you choose. And look at your playmates. As many combinations as there are melodies on a piano."

Chris turns his head to look out at the crowd again, seeing them with new eyes. Realizing what they're all about, his fear diminishes a little.

"I think I understand," he responds. *"But I'm not trying to play games with you, and I'm quite happy with my...pleasure organ. I only want to find my daughter. She was brought here by one of you, one with long fangs that stick up out of its mouth."*

He places his extended fingers in front of his mouth to demonstrate.

There is a long silence in which Chris senses recognition in Banguai.

"Does this individual, by any chance, also have a body like a skinned orangutan?"

The distaste-ridden question sparks a flicker in Chris's spirit.

"Yes. So it is one of yours then."

"Absolutely not. That thing and its mother were here before us. We tried to befriend them, until they abducted one of ours and used them for some sort of experiment. We cut ties with them at that point."

The word 'experiment' sets Chris's teeth on edge.

"Then, you probably didn't know it's figured out how to kidnap people and bring them here."

Her expression darkens. Chris knows he's on the right track.

"It took my daughter. They're here now, somewhere, but I have no idea where to find them. I need you to tell me where they are. If you can do that, I'll do the rest on my own."

Banguai releases a hissing scoff.

"You'd never make it there by yourself. The outside of our little club isn't as hospitable as what you've experienced thus far. Except for Lovely, none of us have ever traveled more than a short distance from here."

"Lovely?"

She gestures toward her four-eared partner.

"My current fling. It's the only one of us actually from this world."

"Would it know where to take me?"

Her face grows stern.

"I'm not inclined to request that of Lovely."

Chris takes a moment, tries to think of any card he can play.

"*Suppose I was to say you owe it to me? As compensation?*"

"*Compensation for what?*"

Chris has to swallow his disgust and force his head to stay in the game.

"*The...whatever it is that brought me down here to you. It attacked me upstairs after I first arrived.*"

"*Revelation attacked you? In what way?*"

Chris grows rigid and hot, but manages to recount the creature's assault.

"*Revelation did this without your agreement?*"

"*That's right. So, the way I see it, it's on you to see to it I didn't come here just for that. Are you going to give me, at the very least, a slight opportunity to rescue my daughter, and a little bit of my dignity in the process?*"

Banguai spends a long moment looking at Chris, considering his words. Then, she summons her eyeless companion with a gesture of her arm.

It saunters up to her side. Banguai takes its head between her hands and speaks to it. It recoils and lowers its head. She kneels and runs her hand along its side, whispering and giving comfort. She stands and addresses Chris.

"*Lovely will guide you to where our flabby acquaintance lives. Never stray from it, and pay attention to the landscape at all times.*"

Lovely approaches and places its snout against Chris's leg, nuzzles it a single time, then descends the platform, waiting for Chris to follow. Chris looks to Banguai.

"*If I find her and get her away from it, how will I get us back to our own world?*"

*"The same way you got here. The question you should
be asking is, how will you get her out of there with your
limbs still attached? If she's even still alive, that is."*

Her last line slices through Chris. He starts to turn,
then he hears her voice again.

*"Don't worry about Revelation, either. Things like that
are taken very seriously here. It will be dealt with."*

"How?" Chris inquires.

Banguai grins.

"We'll use our imaginations."

Chris decides to leave it at that and steps off of the
platform. The crowd of mutants has parted to let him
through.

He follows Lovely across the cavern. The quadruped
beckons him into the spiral tunnel he entered from,
offering its glistening vertebral cord to help with the
climb. Chris reluctantly extends his hand and the spine
wraps around his wrist and pulls him up the twisting
passage. It leads him through the decrepit diner, to an
arched doorway Chris didn't notice before. A crawling
pink mass like a bowl of intestines fills the doorway,
sealing the diner off from the outside.

Lovely pokes its snout around different locations of
the wriggling mass until it finds a smooth port of entry
and shoves its way into the wall of guts. Its hind legs
disappear into the snug opening, which then snaps shut
with a wet belch.

Chris swallows his apprehension—along with the bile
which has risen to his throat—and steps up to the doorway. He reaches out and explores the creases of the warm,
damp barrier until finding a spot where his fingers sink in.
The meat cables create a suction that pulls his arm in
further. Chris orders himself not to resist. The wall swal-

lows all of him: shoulder, head, torso, legs, and ejects him out the other side into still, humid air. He spills onto a hard surface, disoriented.

When everything stops spinning, he lifts his head and looks upon the landscape.

CHAPTER EIGHT

Chris notices the sky first. It has a deep orange color and looks thick enough to stop a bullet. Instead of stars, there are twitching lines of yellow light casting thin rays down, like sodium lamps in a parking lot.

The diner, it turns out, stands in the middle of a valley. Enormous tentacles lie limp across the terrain as far as he can see. The light from above spreads an eerie glow through the low layer of mist floating across the land.

Chris, lying sideways on the huge chunk of black rock the diner stands on, feels dizzy as though from low blood sugar as he takes in the landscape. He spots Lovely taking delicate steps along the tentacled ground. It comes to a halt and turns toward Chris, waiting for him to join.

Lovely is right, Chris decides. There's no time for gazing. He pushes himself to his feet. Knees weak, it takes some wobbling and arm-flapping to steady himself. He descends to the base of the rock, its jagged surface cutting into the bottoms of his feet, but he fights through the pain.

Looking at Lovely, he sees that, although its feet are blurry through the dense fog, they appear not to be sinking into the tentacles at all. There can't be more than a thin layer of them, he concludes, and the ground beneath must be solid.

Confident, he steps off the rock and heads toward his guide. The ground is less sturdy than he assumed—within the first few paces his feet are swallowed to the ankle under the giant tendrils, accompanied by a damp sucking sound. His soles displace a thick layer of sludge that feels to him like wet coffee grounds. It takes a firm yank to pull his foot free and step forward. He does this with the other foot and continues trudging until he's caught up with Lovely.

His companion guides Chris and they make slow progress up the rise in the valley, the close horizon slowly revealing more of the overhead strings of light.

Something crawls over Chris's foot, startling him. He looks down and shudders at the sight of the snake-like body walking on ten pairs of thin legs. He freezes as the critter moves over his other foot and then wanders away.

Chris is ready to collapse from exhaustion by the time they reach the top edge of the valley. When he sees the expanse that still lies ahead, he wants to fall back and let himself sink into the ground—the land stretches out, vast as a desert. What truly unnerves Chris are the openings dotting the terrain, chasms big enough to swallow city blocks and running close enough together that traversing the land in a straight line, no matter what direction Lovely leads him in, will be impossible.

You've gotten this far. You aren't giving up over a couple of holes in the ground.

Eyes returning to the foreground, he sees Lovely has

started off without him, heading away from the direction in which Chris has been looking. Chris commands his body to start moving, too.

It isn't long before they come to one of the cavities in the land and have to change course to go around it. No sooner does it seem they have passed that one than another greets them, and the cycle repeats itself, over and over. The circuitous path becomes torturous for Chris. Little by little, the shock he feels at the bizarre landscape withers away, replaced by gloom and frustration. A resigned numbness takes over by the time he sees a thin pink glow in the distance, pulsing bright to dim like a far-off campfire.

Is that where they're headed, Chris wonders? He thinks he can see some kind of structure behind it, but before Chris can study it for more details, a sound like a cross between steam hissing and the shriek of an eagle comes from somewhere much closer. An alarm goes off inside Chris. He whips his head in the direction it came from, but sees nothing.

Another scream erupts, echoing. In the corner of his eye, he sees Lovely turning its whole body toward the noise. Then, it walks up to Chris and lays on its stomach a few feet away from him, swiveling its head from Chris to the source of the sound and back. It stretches itself out along the ground, then begins to disappear. The strands of fur covering it morph into tentacles like those resting across the terrain until it is only with sharp eyes that Chris can make out its shape among the alien pasture.

Camouflage. Whatever is making the noise, Lovely doesn't want to be seen by it. Crunching sounds start to echo, and then he sees the source of the noises climb out from one of the holes in the land. He understands now why his companion has hidden itself.

Five upside-down sets of antlers moving together in a mass the size of a building are crawling across the land. It would appear spider-like if not for the smaller horns branching out from its main limbs. The crunching noise Chris heard is caused by the bending of the horns as they lift and fall into the ground in tandem with each other.

It is moving away from Chris until one of the tiny reptiles wanders too close, letting out short hisses. The giant, bone-white leg closest to it rises off the ground and one of its sharp ends falls back into it, stabbing the tiny reptile just below its head. It lifts its catch to the top of its body, where five of what look to Chris like the giant worm tongues from the movie *Tremors* spring out and devour it piece by piece. It's gone in several seconds. The worm tongues all open their mouths wide and seem to scout the area around them. One of them stops, its open maw facing Chris dead-on. A rapid clicking sound escapes it. All of the other worm tongues turn to face Chris. The larger antler body begins moving toward him.

Oh, fuck.

Cold terror floods Chris's brain. He pictures his corpse being digested, leaving Tara's fate in Red Fang's hands. He looks to where Lovely has camouflaged itself. He decides to test his own abilities in this world and try joining it, knowing he'll be dead if he's wrong.

Chris lies down on his stomach, head turned to the side with his cheek against the slick tentacles, forearm close to his eyes. He focuses on the texture and hue of his flesh and imagines it transforming. Narrowing his focus, forcing the monster's approach from his thoughts, he visualizes tentacles like those under him growing out of his pores.

Then, it starts happening for real, or at least it appears that way. Chris doesn't feel anything growing from him, realizes it's all illusion. He almost loses focus, but hearing the crunch of legs moving, much closer now, he renews his concentration. He closes his eye and pictures tentacles growing out all over him, covering his hospital gown, arms, legs, and head.

The ground under him rattles from the advancing steps. Chris feels the moving statue of bone standing right over him. He opens his eye just a slit to get a look at his forearm. It appears as though it's been buried under a mound of tentacles, hiding it.

Chris holds the illusion as best he can, waiting for something to happen or not happen. The antler limbs make wet sounds piercing through tentacles and the sludge beneath, on one side of him at first and then on all sides. He hears the worm appendages clicking back and forth between each other from a story above him.

Realizing he's forgotten to breathe, he resists the urge to gasp, instead letting the air in slow and quiet. The brittle grinding starts up again, the legs of his pursuer returning to their former pace. One of its back legs penetrates the ground only a foot or so from Chris's head, causing him to jump, but he holds his focus and keeps himself hidden as the monster edges away. He hears it stop several times, followed by the high shrieks of the legged snakes being eaten. The sounds of the steps gradually change to something rockier, with more of an echo. He looks in the direction the noise comes from and sees the antler body at a distance, climbing down into one of the cavernous holes.

He waits until the sounds have faded, then releases the mental grip he's held. The illusory tentacles vanish. It takes a moment for his brain to start working normally again. It occurs to him to get up. Pushing himself back to a standing position, Chris remembers he's not alone—he looks toward where he saw Lovely lay down and sees it return to its own natural form. It stands up and, as though nothing has happened, starts back in the direction it was leading Chris. Still shaken from the close call, he steers his focus to the small pink line on the horizon. The burden of the great distance reasserts itself in his tired bones. He takes a deep breath and moves to catch up with his strange guide.

Chris's legs feel like hot iron after their trek. The siren sound he heard back near the diner has grown louder and clearer, a choir of screams packing his head to near-shattering, even with his fingers in his ears. He and Lovely have reached their destination.

What appeared as a vague pool of neon at the beginning of the journey is now visible as a pink lake of fog, much thicker than the white mist they've waded through this whole time. At its center sits an island of the same shiny black rock as the diner, rising out of the haze, its half-moon shape making it look to Chris like a crumbled sphinx spreading monstrous arms out toward them.

"Is she in there?" Chris asks Lovely, not averting his eyes from the megalith.

Lovely responds by putting a foot forward and starting into the mist. Chris follows. The mass becomes more detailed as they get closer, until Chris makes out the source of the deafening howls. They come from the countless figures covering the side of the rock, shapes of children's bodies jutting out as though pressing against tight-drawn silk—legs and arms flailing, mouths stretched into horrific O's.

The sight, worse than anything Chris has seen in this world, the antler-being included, makes him tremble. He realizes his steps have slowed to sporadic paces. A surge of shame follows.

Still with the self-preservation act. Tara is in there, somewhere, and the slower you go the more likely you are to find her too late.

Chris knows his inner voice is right. Time to haul ass. Chris jogs toward the crescent rock, passing Lovely. He enters the crag's extended arms and continues until its center face blocks out the orange sky, drowning Chris in shadow. He pauses and looks around for an entrance, expecting some high jagged archway like in an Indiana Jones movie, but sees none. The only apertures he can see in the wailing rock are narrow tunnel openings scattered at different points and heights along the rock face. From all of them, some kind of gelatinous substance, like the contents of a neglected grease trap, dribbles out, hanging in gooey streams down the bluff.

He feels a tug on the bottom of his hospital gown, looks down, and sees Lovely pulling on the fabric with its mouth.

"Lead the way, Lovely," he says.

He follows it toward the nearest-to-ground level of the substance-drooling passageways. The rancid smell grows stronger the closer they get. Lovely stops at the entryway and looks back and forth between it and Chris.

Stifling a gag, Chris peers inside. Gelatinous slop,

alive and squirming, rises diagonally from a low ebb to the ceiling of the tunnel.

Lovely climbs in, feet slipping in the muck, using its back legs to push itself the rest of the way in. It stops and looks back, urging Chris to join. He fights his hesitation, braces himself, kneels down, and reaches in, grabbing a handful of Lovely's long gangly fur. Crawling in, the sludge feels as disgusting as he thought it would. The further in he gets, using one hand and both legs to crawl while holding on to Lovely with the other hand, the higher the goop rises along his body, first to his elbows, then up to his shoulders, then his neck.

He takes a nauseated breath and goes all the way under. Prepared to experience a growing ache in his lungs from lack of oxygen, and to hurry like hell through the sludge to reach open air, he is surprised to find, after a minute or so, he feels no urge to inhale or exhale.

They make slow progress. Chris senses the turns, rises, and dips in the narrow space. It occurs to him the whole inside of the rock might be filled with this goop. If so, he wonders, how will be able to see to find Tara—or to fight Red Fang, if necessary? He supposes he'll just have to improvise and hope for the best, just as he's done up to this point.

Lovely comes to a stop and jerks itself away from Chris. He hears the gooey noise of it turning around, feels its mouth close around his wrist and, for a terrifying second, is convinced he's been had, that Banguai sent him into this forsaken space to be mauled and eaten, bones left to putrefy and become one with the sludge.

But Lovely doesn't bite. Its grip stays firm but considerate as it tugs Chris's arm to a spot along the side of the tunnel, a divot in the otherwise solid surface. Chris explores it by touch and finds he can reach his fingers in, like a handle in a floorboard hidey hole.

He feels Lovely's form slide against him as it winds around his body, heading in the direction they came from. Chris realizes he's been left to his own devices. Perhaps his guide was only instructed to take him this far, or maybe it's scared of Red Fang and whatever else may wait beyond this point. He can't blame it.

Either way, he's on his own now, and wondering what the hell he's supposed to do with this crack in the wall.

He collects himself and thinks.

He thinks of the way he dealt with the monster that came after him on the way here, making himself appear to become a part of his surroundings. What if he tries to go further, and actually turn himself into the sludge around him? He could squeeze through the crack like ketchup out of a bottle.

Chris realizes, if this is going to work, he'll need to push his mental willpower much further than he has up till now. He gets on all fours, getting into the proper head space, clearing his mind, turning himself into a blank vessel. He studies the texture and smell of the sludge. Opens his mouth and breathes its taste. He swallows mouthful after mouthful of it, forcing his perception of his body to align with its dank pungent flavor and creeping texture. He pictures his skin undergoing the physical and chemical changes in phases.

His material self putrefies and loses solvency. His skin and the layers of the tissue beneath turn gelatinous. Chris withers and joins the plasma, becoming an area of encompassing mass—a location with consciousness.

Chris lets himself drip and churn through the rest of the sludge, down toward the crack in the floor. He forces a glob of himself through the crack, and then more, feels himself bubble and spread like an oil leak on the other side of the opening, until the last of him comes free with a sickening *pthwup*.

Having made it through the hole, Chris begins the work of reassembling his old self. The process takes longer than he hoped, leaving him depleted and weak on the ground. He doesn't move or think until a few stray chuckles come up from his chest and rise to a crescendo of mad laughter. His body quakes, causing the rough ground under him to poke and punch his naked back, the hospital gown lost to the sludge tunnel.

Pain brings awareness back into him like shy ribbons of smoke. He sits up—too quickly, it turns out, and falls back, hitting his head. Pain explodes in his bad eye. He wants only to sleep and dream about sleeping and never ever move his exhausted body again, but he knows that's not an option. Putting his palms on the gritty floor, he pushes himself up and beholds his fresh hell.

At first glance, the cave duct is the most mentally digestible place he's seen since the hospital. The silence helps. He can hear the blood pumping through his body.

A curved ceiling of ash-colored rock stares down at him. He wonders how, with no apparent light source, he is able to see anything. It comes to him as he studies the rock walls. There are flecks and spatters of white, like caulking, which glow with a strange luminescence.

Where the hell do I go from here? he wonders.

He supposes he'll have to wander until he comes upon something.

Wait a minute, he thinks. *Maybe not.*

He begins thinking about all of the encounters he had with Red Fang back in his own world. It never had to look for Chris. It always knew where he would be and could just show up, right there.

Why? According to Red Fang, it was because the fucker had managed to sniff out Chris's link to this world and attach itself to it, and therefore to Chris himself.

It should work the other way around, Chris figures. He'll hone in on Red Fang's frequency—which shouldn't be too different from the sludge trick he just performed—and, hopefully, flicker out of his current location, showing up wherever Tara's being kept.

But what, then? Are you going to announce you're there to collect your daughter and the thing will say

'Oh, yes, absolutely!'

Shake your hand with that gargoyle claw and send you both on your way?

Chris considers this. "You're right," he says. "I'll have to figure out some way I can fight that thing."

Good idea. Go toe-to-toe with a seven-foot hell beast, that'll work out beautifully. Or, let me guess your next idea —you'll just go in there and improvise your way out, like you've done all the way up to now. Because, of course, luck never runs out, does it?

Chris slumps his shoulders, realizing the voice has him pegged—and that talking to oneself doesn't always speak well of one's sanity.

To have the slimmest chance of saving Tara and getting her back to their own world, he knows he'll have to form some sort of strategy.

But where to start? What's available to him?

He thinks back on his encounters with Red Fang, remembering what it did and said. Its talk about Chris's own link to this dimension, and how it attached itself to it to get to Tara. Maybe he can use that somehow.

But first, he needs to test this.

Turning over ideas on how to do this, he hits on one that seems doable. It would be nice if he had time to rest and get his head back into a good place before attempting it, but by this point he doubts anything less than a month's worth of sleep would accomplish that. He'll have to make do with what little fuel is left in him.

He closes his eyes and silences his mind, taking slow and steady breaths. When he is relaxed and empty, he allows the single image of Red Fang to appear in the darkness behind his eyes.

Tamping down his rage at the sight of his enemy is harder than he thought, but Chris reminds himself of the stakes. He completes the visualization and holds it, giving it weight and solidity. Then, he imagines the image dissolving and losing shape. It becomes a thick fog of glistening crimson, which Chris expands so his whole brain is enveloped in it.

The red cloud dissipates and reveals a new space. Chris finds himself looking at a moving picture, something like a virtual reality experience. The same illuminated rock as the tunnel he's standing in fills the corners of his vision, framing a raised slab on which Red Fang is lying.

No, Chris realizes, it's not Red Fang. This thing is shorter and wider, with features that are slightly different from his enemy's, the eye slits longer and the upward fangs set closer together. He remembers Red Fang's references to "Mama". An intubation tube-like implement, made of material resembling tapeworm skin, runs out of this monster's mouth, to the side, and out of sight.

Chris's eyes fly open and he grabs his forehead. The piercing ache in his skull, building the longer he holds the connection, becoming too much. He feels a tickle around one of his nostrils, wipes at his nose, and brings his fingers away dabbed with blood.

He allows himself to rest until he can think straight, but is encouraged knowing for sure he can link up to Red Fang's consciousness.

Recovered, Chris considers how he can use the link to his advantage. On its own, it won't help much. He brainstorms. Maybe there are things he can do in combination with this ability. He shudders, thinking of the effort and strain that would involve, but doesn't allow himself to back away from the train of thought.

After some contemplation and imagining, Chris comes upon one possibility. He closes his eyes and projects himself into Red Fang's mind again. Red Fang has left Mama's side and approached what looks like a half-shell made of fossilized maggots. It reaches into the improvised bowl, into what reminds Chris of YouTube footage of an endoscopy, brings out a full claw, and raises the contents to its mouth. Chris pushes his revulsion away and focuses on the background. With laser focus, he visualizes a small creature, the size of a rat or a gerbil, scuttling rapidly across the floor and out of sight.

Red Fang jerks its head toward the movement, as Chris hoped it would. Seeing nothing, it turns and looks around the room, allowing Chris to get its full layout. The slab on which Mama is lying is in the center of the space.

Against the wall, in the background behind the slab, Chris sees Tara for the first time since she was taken from him.

Unconscious, she is bound in a standing position by thick vines wrapped around her wrists, ankles, forehead, and midsection. The other end of the tube running out of

Mama and along the ground rises up to Tara's blue lips. Her skin looks as though it's coated in gray flour.

Chris loses his connection as an atom bomb of emotion goes off inside him, and collapses to the jagged ground. He wants to go right back in and physically crawl through the mental link he's established, tear his way out of Red Fang's head, and rush over to her.

Realizing he'll be no good to her in this state, he forces himself to calm down and focus on the intelligence he's gathered. Now, he knows the layout of the room where Tara is being held. He can invade Red Fang's head, as well as create illusions within it. Most of the tools are there—enough of them, at least, to start building a plan.

He rubs his eyes and forehead, wipes a fresh dribble of blood from his nose, and wonders, *Okay, what will step one need to be?*

CHAPTER NINE

Chris builds his plan, piece by piece, while traversing the network of tunnels in the rock structure. He's decided to find Tara and Red Fang on foot, as rough as the ground is, to give his brain time to rest and recharge. A workable scenario is in place in Chris's head by the time he rounds a curve in the tunnel network and a side opening comes into view.

Chris comes to a quick halt, backs out of view, and cranes his head around. The glow from the entryway's threshold is brighter than in the rest of the cave, throwing a warped pool of light against the opposite wall. Chris passed a number of other side pockets like this while wandering the maze, but no more light came from them than lit the main corridors.

He decides he needs to be sure before getting his hopes up. The floor of the cave has tortured Chris's feet enough that his steps have been light and slow for a while, but he makes them even more deliberate as he paces toward the entryway. He stops a yard from where the glow streams out, gets just close enough to view a small section of the chamber. He is able to see the container from his previous vision which held whatever the hell Red Fang was eating. His heart bounces against his ribs as he takes a few more steps. The edge of the slab on which Mama lies inches into view, followed by the monster's clawed feet and lower legs.

This is it, Chris thinks.

His mouth becomes drier than it already was. If this doesn't work, not only will his chance to save Tara slip through his fingers, but he'll certainly die at Red Fang's hands. It crosses his mind that the father he was back in their driveway, the guy who froze in terror while thinking his daughter was being killed, probably wouldn't have made it this close.

Don't pat yourself on the back. You're still the same terrified man you were then. Real question is if you can grit your teeth through the fear long enough to see this through.

He backs up further and disappears behind the curve. After taking a moment to gather all of his mental energy, Chris closes his eyes and begins step one of his plan.

Placing himself back into Red Fang's head, he sees the monster lifting a claw full of the meat to its mouth. Chris holds onto the connection as tight as he can. He practiced the trick in small ways while walking the cave, but this will be the first time he's done it while linked to Red Fang. He opens his mouth, takes a giant breath in, and yells as loudly as he can—"Hey!"

It works. Instead of coming from his own mouth, Chris's voice echoes from down the tunnel on the other side of the chamber entry. Right away, he sees the moving picture in Red Fang's eyes jerk up and over, looking out into the corridor. Red Fang stands in a hurry and rushes out into the tunnel. It looks in Chris's direction, where he's hidden just out of sight, and then the other way.

Chris yells "Down here!" and Red Fang, hearing the words from the opposite direction, breaks into a clumsy sprint down the tunnel, away from Chris and the chamber.

Now that he's sent the bastard away, it's time for Chris to keep the goose chase going. In Red Fang's vision, he sees the glowing walls of the tunnel rushing by on all sides. A forked path in the cave approaches. That will be perfect, Chris decides. He focuses harder, ignores the crushing pain in his skull, and creates an image to place in Red Fang's sights.

As the fork gets closer, the figure—a replica of Chris himself—appears in the left corridor. Chris pictures his avatar turning its back on Red Fang and running. Red Fang takes the bait and picks up speed, entering the tunnel after it.

Satisfied he's put enough distance between Red Fang and the chamber, Chris shifts to the next step of the plan —getting in the chamber and getting Tara. He needs to keep the illusion going, so he keeps his eyes shut and feels his way along the tunnel walls while the image of the chase plays on a closed circuit in his head. The dissonance threatens to shatter his brain, but he keeps going.

His balance falters, so he sidles up to and props himself against the rock and slides along it. When he reaches the entryway, the sudden opening causes him to stumble and nearly lose his concentration. He reattaches himself to the wall and slides into the chamber as if he's balancing on a ledge.

A flare of excitement rises in him, realizing he's in the same room as his daughter again. It grows as he moves closer to where he knows she's tied up. It explodes like fireworks when his hand bumps against Tara's.

Chris has been focused for so long on getting her back again that he wants to rest. He knows better, though. He keeps himself in Red Fang's head and keeps it running, choking back his urge to celebrate.

Moving his hand blindly up Tara's arm, Chris feels the vines holding her in place. Searching her face, his fingertips touch the tube running from her mouth to Mama's. Its length feels taut and fleshy, like a full water balloon. He wonders if it would break if he tried to pull it out of Tara's throat. Would that hurt her?

Chris decides to remove the tube at Mama's end, instead. Preparing to walk away from the wall, sightless, he realizes he is holding Tara's hand. His fingers instinctively squeeze her palm tighter. He doesn't want to let go, wants no more distance between them, not even the few feet he is about to travel.

Just a few more minutes. You're almost home. Get it done.

Chris turns his back to the wall and leans against it. He gives Tara's hand one last squeeze, then releases it. Placing one foot out in front of him, he feels as though he's about to step off a cliff. If he trips or bumps into something, the connection might be broken. Red Fang realizing it's been chasing a phantom would cut Chris's time down, which is the last thing he needs.

Step lightly, he tells himself, and then breaks away from the wall. He checks each upcoming step with his toes before planting his feet down, and in this way makes slow progress, hoping he's going in the right direction.

Chris sees, through Red Fang's eyes, that its speed is beginning to dwindle. It's getting tired.

His big toe taps the side of something. He extends his arms in front of him, palms facing out, and bends over until his hands land on something with the girth and texture of a dead fish. Chris recognizes it from when Red Fang grabbed him before. He's propping himself up on Mama's arm. A quick stab of dread, but he recovers when he feels no response from the sleeping monster. The revulsion caused by having his skin against the cold flesh remains.

As he did with Tara, Chris slides his palm up the monster's arm and around the shoulder until he reaches the face, which is smooth and squishy like waterlogged wood. His fingers arrive at the tube connecting Mama to his daughter. It goes up alongside its jaw and enters at the corner of the mouth, snaking in under the upward-growing fangs.

Chris stands upright for better leverage and gathers the tube in both hands, gripping it at the entrance to Mama's mouth. He tugs gently and the tube stretches a little but there is resistance and he squeezes more firmly, using his whole upper body to pull on the cable. Sensing the line is stretching thin, he pauses and then eases himself back a little more. There is a soft rustle like soggy paper being squeezed and Chris feels a few inches of the tube slide free from Mama's throat. He doesn't allow himself to celebrate but instead gives another slow pull. The tube comes loose a little more.

Sliding his hand back to Mama's mouth along the tube, he feels it has narrowed to a dime's width. Confident he's found the proper rhythm to remove it all the way, Chris starts pulling once more, which is when the tube shatters and he flies back, landing on his ass. His good eye flies open on its own, and he sees a small portion of something like black ink landing on his feet and legs like expelled blood. Mama's mouth snaps open and lets loose a gurgling hiss that fills the cave room like a siren. It seizes and convulses on the rock bed, limbs flailing.

It dawns on Chris that he's no longer riding in Red Fang's head. He slams his eyes shut, ignoring the screams, and when he sees through Red Fang's eyes again he sees the monster is standing still and looking at the empty tunnel in front of it. It turns its head sideways, as though listening to something. It seems to recognize what the sound is, turns around and runs back the way it came, a hissing roar escaping its mouth.

Chris, reopening his eye, finds his brain heavy from being in the same place as his body again, like stepping on dry ground after swimming awhile. Willing his arms to obey, he pushes himself up, turns around, and staggers across the room toward Tara. He planned on getting her to a safe place where there would be time for him to recharge before carrying out the final step in his plan. Now he'll have to make do with the few seconds he has.

Chris places his weak hands on either side of her face and his forehead against hers. He hopes what got him over to this dimension will get him back to his own, Tara with him. Focusing on the point where their heads touch, he envisions his daughter as an extension of himself, a child-shaped limb attached to his brain. He allows himself to start sinking into his mind, the chamber dissolving from his awareness.

It comes flying back as Chris is wrenched away from Tara, the thick-knuckled red claw snapping round his throat from behind and lifting him off his feet, craning him around and slamming him into the wall by his daughter, the impact igniting his shoulder blades. Red Fang, once again crushing his windpipe, releases a torrent of breath from its roaring, open-stretched mouth that stings Chris's face like freezing rain.

A moment passes in which he expects to close his eyes and open them to a chamber without Red Fang, his head still against Tara's, but after he blinks he's still being strangled against the wall.

This is how it ends?

He decides if he's going to die now, he doesn't want the last image he sees to be of Red Fang. With the claw squeezing so tightly, Chris can only manage to swivel his head a few inches to the side, not enough to get a look at his daughter. He settles for reaching out and feeling around until he finds her restricted hand.

The cut-off blood flow makes his head feel as though a semi-truck has parked on top of it. His vision starts to blur and his limbs lose strength. His hand grows tingly until he's too weak to hold Tara's any longer. His fingers unclasp and slip away.

The broken contact causes a change in Chris. A low unexpected hum flows through him, electric and hot and fueled by looking into Red Fang's obsidian eyes.

Hate.

It swells in his muscles like venom. The hopelessness of seconds ago turns to something blind and snarling. He imagines a pair of antlers emerging from his temples and piercing through Red Fang's eyes and forehead at bullet speed, pushing brain and skull out the back.

Coming up behind this image is the recollection of the antlered beast Chris evaded on his journey to the cave. An idea rides on the back of the memory.

Weak but newly driven, he lifts his hands to Red Fang's face. In one rapid movement his thumbs find the slitted eyes and plunge into their firm slickness, sinking down to the second knuckle. A howl like a shotgun blast explodes from Red Fang's mouth, but its grip on Chris's throat stays firm.

He closes his eyes and, as he was about to do with Tara, puts everything into envisioning their surroundings changing. Instead of his home world, though, he thinks of the tentacled land between here and the diner. The effort sends blades of agony through his head, but he bullies himself into continuing. The hard surface against his back softens and he briefly feels himself sinking as though into crumbling adobe, and then there is nothing behind him and he is tumbling backward, landing on a bed of thick membranous extremities which do not absorb the impact of Red Fang's body falling onto him. The row of fangs smacks him like a pitchfork and causes blood to flow from his mouth. But, the claw is no longer around his throat, and he fills his lungs with air, crying out as a cracked rib explodes with pain.

Red Fang yanks its head away, Chris's thumbs leaving its destroyed eye matter with a pulpy *schlup*. It rolls off him and falls on its back, howling. It rolls again and pushes itself onto hands and knees. Chris drags himself out of its reach.

He scans the terrain and locates the nearest chasm in the landscape. He backs up toward it, letting out a cry of pain. Not much acting is required.

"My leg!" he yells. It comes out ragged and not as loud as he'd planned.

Red Fang turns in Chris's direction and lets out an enraged roar. Now blind, it tries to wade through the field of tentacles. It trips and falls forward. Frustrated grunts escape its mouth.

"What is this?" Red Fang feels around. *"Where have you brought me?"*

It surprises Chris that his enemy doesn't recognize the strange dead flora, even by touch. It must have forgotten life outside those rock walls.

"Owww, fuck!" Chris says, backing slowly toward the giant hole.

Red Fang pushes itself up cautiously and tests the ground in front of him before each step.

"Save your screams. Whatever pain you're in, you'll beg for it while I tear you apart one little piece at a time!"

Red Fang is quick in adapting to the odd terrain. It's gait gains confidence and speed.

"No, stay away!" He backs up slow, letting the monster get closer to his voice. "I'll do whatever you want. Don't hurt me!"

Chris's pleading makes Red Fang advance harder. He reaches the edge of the hole.

"No, please! No!"

He holds steady as Red Fang breaks into a ferocious semi-sprint and then leaps forward. Chris turns and dives out of the way. On the ground, he turns and looks toward the hole, catching a glimpse of Red Fang disappearing into the abyss.

A howl of panic follows, growing fainter until it seems to come from a mile down. Chris crawls to the edge and hears the yell joined by a familiar crackle like breaking branches. The howl of panic turns to a shriek of terror and agony, and then goes quiet.

Chris, shaking, continues listening. The trauma of these last hours has him certain this can't be the end, that Red Fang is tricking him and is about to leap up from the darkness of the hole and finish its job like a slasher in a horror movie.

But the silence doesn't break.

Chris rolls over on his back and lies staring at the orange sky, uncomprehending as a newborn, no thoughts forming. He stays supine for a long while and over the course of many minutes—possibly hours—his mind rebuilds itself until he remembers where he is and why he is there.

Realizing he'll have to break his brain further, just a little bit more, to get back to Tara and get them back to their world makes his stomach wobble. He turns on his side and dry heaves. But then, he accepts it, closes his eyes, and returns to his daughter to get them back home.

CHAPTER TEN

"No window broken in his room, and he couldn't have snuck past the nurse's station."

Officer Hayden shakes her head. "Nope. I had security take me through the footage of the nurse's station, the hallway to the elevators, everything. Plus, his assigned nurse had been in his room to check on him just before he barricaded his door. When we busted in there, he was gone."

Deputy Sheriff Kelso chews the inside of his cheek and looks at the carpeted floor. "He was pretty banged up when you rode in with him?"

"In and out of consciousness, talking nonsense. Funny thing is, they didn't find any brain impact, and his tox report is clean. Could be a psychotic episode."

"Well, he didn't tunnel his way out of there. We'll keep everything locked down for now and hope he shows up. If it turns out he did something to that girl, I want him in chains, episode or no episode."

"Think we should have a grief counselor ready when the wife gets here?"

"I have one on the phone with her now. It's a long ride down here from Grand Rapids, even longer in the passenger seat of a police car. Don't want—"

"HEY!"

A male nurse comes tearing down the hallway, eyes wide with shock.

"There's...you gotta..."

The nurse stops trying to speak and gestures wildly for the two cops to return to the Intensive Care ward.

The officer tasked with keeping guard over the room Chris vanished from has backed away from the door and stands frozen, jaw about down to his chest. Kelso lifts his hand to the holster on his belt, ready to draw, and treads into the hospital room.

He places his hand on the shoulder of Nurse Elson and sidles around her.

What in God's holy name?

He approaches the bed, where a lifeless-looking girl with something trailing out of her mouth and dangling off the side of the mattress is lying. Getting closer, he sees a hand holding the girl's. The one-eyed man in a gown sitting on the floor beside the bed come fully into view. He has the glazed look of a boxer at the end of a brutal match.

"Nurse," Kelso says, "check this girl, *now.*"

Nurse Elson does as instructed, approaching the bed and placing her fingers to the girl's wrist.

"There's a pulse."

Kelso hears the man whisper something, but it's too low to make out. He keeps his hand near his firearm, just in case, and kneels down to him.

In a ravaged voice, Chris rasps, "Help her."

CHAPTER ELEVEN

Two Days Later

Chris is watching TV from one of the leather chairs in his hospital room, resisting the severe urge to rub at his gauze eye patch, when Chelsea walks in. She stands at the bed curtain for a moment, taking in the sight of him, then approaches. Chris is about to say "That bad, huh?" to break the ice, but closes his mouth, deciding to wait and see which way the wind is blowing with her.

"You look like a bomb exploded in your face," Chelsea says.

She lowers herself into the chair across the small table from Chris. Her arms need a moment to decide what to do with themselves. When they settle on a locked-finger pose across her lap, it looks stiff and unnatural.

"You look like you haven't slept in three days," Chris says, his face drifting in and out of a half-smile.

"I can't imagine why." She points to the empty food tray next to the hospital bed. "Is that as nasty as it looks?"

"Did you notice how much is left on there?"

Chelsea forces a chuckle that's more of *hmm*, then the low sound of the TV is all there is.

"So, are you going to tell me why you're in here and Tara is two floors up, eating yogurt and Jell-O, barely able to talk above a whisper? Why cops and social workers have been grilling me about you and our home life for the past two days?"

Chris makes himself keep eye contact and hides his sudden hunger for breath. He did the same when he lied to the sheriff, Kelso. But then, it was the stakes of not losing Tara and/or being confined to a cell, concrete or padded, that drove his anxiety. Now, it's the guilt of deceiving Chelsea that's affecting him like raw sewage under his skin.

"Someone took her."

"Took her?"

"When I crashed the car. I was taking her to Brianna's for a little while—a writer I know online was doing a signing and reading at The Mystery Box and I thought I'd show up."

Which was partially true. He'd seen his online acquaintance's social media posts about the event, but had been too engaged in sulking over his own failure to bother with it.

"You didn't say anything to me about that," Chelsea says.

"It was a spur of the moment thing. I don't know. Trying to be spontaneous for once."

Chelsea stares, waiting for the rest of the story.

"It was dark and raining. I didn't see the guy standing in the road. All of a sudden, something hits the windshield and smashes a hole right in front of me. Rock or something. The glass goes in my eye and next thing I know the car is plowing into the neighbor's house."

Chris wishes like hell Chelsea's eyes would betray something. Give him a hint of softness or anger. But they remain neutral, no doubt intentional. It's part of why Chris fell in love with her. She's the most controlled human being he's ever known.

But right now it's not helping him any.

"The last thing I remember seeing is him grabbing her out of her seat and taking off. I got out to try and chase them but I was so fucked up I couldn't see which way they went."

"They said you were crawling around on the hood of the car when the ambulance came, talking like you were drunk."

"Wouldn't surprise me, I guess, but I don't remember."

The long breath Chelsea takes in and releases is the only blip in her demeanor.

"So you don't remember anything else that came after?"

Chris shakes his head, his eyes zipping away from Chelsea and then back, cursing himself for it.

"That's the funny part for me. Someone took Tara, and yet she's here in the hospital now. You don't remember how she was gotten back, and no one else wants to tell me, and when I push the issue they say it's still under investigation. What am I not being told, Chris?"

Chris has rehearsed his response several times, the sudden change in demeanor from confiding to bewildered. He surprises himself by making the switch perfectly.

"Apparently, I disappeared from my hospital room for a couple of hours."

"Disappeared? As in you left the hospital?"

"No, disappeared as in 'poof, he's gone'. I couldn't have gotten out except by going out the door, down the elevator, and through the halls. The nurses would have seen me walk out and the cameras would have filmed me leaving. But they didn't. Yet, they look in my room and I'm not there. Then, two hours later, I'm back, and Tara is with me."

For once, Chelsea looks away, taking in what's been laid out. When she speaks, she builds her sentences with precision, one painstaking phrase at a time.

"So, let me get this straight. Tara was kidnapped. You were able to get her back, despite not knowing who took her or where they went. You left the hospital to get her and then came back, but without actually ever leaving."

"I know how crazy it all sounds. I really wish I could tell you what happened, but everything between the crash and the next morning is just totally blank."

Chelsea looks at him, then relaxes her shoulders. Bitter amusement falls across her face.

"I was almost ready to throw my hands up and go along with you, even with your eyebrows jumping around this whole time. But 'really' and 'totally' in the same sentence? I'm not pretending to be that dumb. It's bullshit that you don't remember anything, isn't it?"

Chris straightens in his seat, lets out a wounded scoff, and prepares to object. But his posturing is weak against his own self-disgust and Chelsea's sharp gaze. He sags back into his chair and lets his eyes go to ground, affirming Chelsea's words and giving a twitch of a nod for good measure.

"Well?" Chelsea says, inviting him to continue.

"One day, I'll tell you everything."

"One day?"

"I know it's not fair to you. But after everything that happened that day, it's a miracle I'm still alive and still sane. Even if I could put words to it, which I'm not sure I can, the truth is I just don't want to go back through it, not for a long time."

"I don't care. Do it anyway."

He looks her in the eyes, into a gaze that's more unyielding than ever, and this time meets it without breaking contact, his own stare apologetic but firm.

"I promise I will tell you everything one day. For right now, I can tell you that Tara was in danger and now she's safe because of me. That's not me taking pride in anything I did, I'm just saying that's what you do for your child and I did it. I know things are up in the air now, with everyone thinking I was the one who put her in that hospital bed, but it could have been a lot worse. I can't order you to be happy with that or even accept it. I can only ask you to give me some time."

"And if I decide I don't want you around Tara while you 'take your time'?"

The notion hits Chris like a brick to the gut, even though he's known the possibility.

"Right now, I just want to make sure she gets to go home when she leaves here. If you decide that me not being there will raise those odds, I won't fight it."

Chelsea retains her composure but can't stop her chest from shuddering up and down as she looks away from Chris, watching the sky out the window. Chris looks away, too, up at the painting of the bird.

CHAPTER TWELVE

Chris shuts his door and waits for Cassie as she treads the salt and slush of the parking lot, walking around the car to join him. The cold air makes his eye socket ache beneath his patch, but he's lived with the pain long enough to push it into the background.

Cassie looks at Tara through the window. "She looks like we're dropping her off at a slaughterhouse."

Chris nods. "She's been staring at the back of my seat the whole ride. She's scared."

Cassie throws an expectant glance toward him, as if to say *You could make all of this easier for me.* He feels a prick of guilt, knowing it's true. But he's nowhere near that point yet, and Cassie grudgingly doesn't push. Opening the rear passenger door, he wishes he could give her a gold medal for her patience.

Cassie leans into the car. "I bet you're super excited to see this place again, aren't you? Be with your friends again, use every paintbrush in the art room." She reaches around and unbuckles her from the car seat. "What do you say? Let's get you back to it."

She holds her hand out for Tara to grab. Tara refuses it, slides her arms crossed, and tucks her chin down.

Chris squeezes Cassie's shoulder. "Mind if I give it a go?"

A silent exchange passes between them. She backs out of the car and stands upright, gesturing him to go right ahead. He gently closes the door, walks around to the other side, and gets in the back seat.

Chris decides they can do without words for a bit. He looks down at the seat between him and Tara, at a children's book from the library called *The Worst Breakfast,* and leafs through the illustrated pages. He knows if he chances a look toward her now, Tara will double down on closing him off.

Chris hears a short rustling come from Tara's winter coat—the sound of her folded arms loosening, just a little. A few more moments and they loosen again, the shuffle trailed by a huff and a sigh. Chris closes the book and lifts his head, looks between the front seats and through the windshield.

"Did I ever tell you how, on my first day of kindergarten, Grandma had to come and take me home early? They had to call her because, as soon as she'd dropped me off, I went into the classroom closet to hide and wouldn't come out. I cried so hard in there that I couldn't breathe, so at one point I actually ended up fainting. My teacher and the guidance counselor heard me stop making noise and had to open the door and pull me out. Grandma came and took me home. I thought it meant I'd never have to go to school again. But, the next day, I was right back in that classroom, crying my eyes out."

"Grandma was mean."

"That's what I thought. But then, you know what

happened? The crying stopped eventually, and I saw how nice my teacher was, and how all the other kids were making friends with each other, and I decided to try and be part of it. After a few days, whenever it was time for the school day to be done, I'd wish it didn't have to end."

"But, I'm not starting school. I was just away so my throat and breathing would get better again."

"Oh, yeah, that's right. And you already have friends you play with at recess, don't you? Like Adelaide and Kaylee."

She nodded.

"And you liked Ms. Klinger when you met her, right?"

Another, more enthusiastic nod.

"And once you're caught back up, you'll be able to go back to Mrs. Dean's class and be with your friends again. Doesn't that sound good?"

"Yeah, I guess." She seems to contemplate something before offering what's on her mind. "But, I don't want to be away from you if the ghost comes back."

There it is, Chris thinks. He figured as much.

Tara, who experienced Red Fang as an invisible attacker, and who remained unconscious during her captivity in the other world, has decided the entity that lifted her off the floor and pulled her through the smashed windshield was a ghost like the ones she'd seen on numerous Halloween episodes of her favorite cartoons. The belief comes with its own nightmares, but Chris finds it preferable to explaining what actually occurred.

"It hasn't come back so far. I think that ghost is pretty much done with us."

"Maybe it's just waiting until I'm all alone."

"You won't be alone, though, and Ms. Klinger seems

like she could take on a ghost just as well as I could. She'll be with you the whole time, and it'll just be a couple of hours. What do you say? Can we just give it a try?"

Tara shakes her head, the words barely out of Chris's mouth.

He tries to find another path of persuasion, but comes up empty. His nicotine cravings bubble up and he holds his breath, imagining his lungs full of smoke until the urge tapers off a bit.

"All right, then," he says, and pushes the door back open. Walking back around the car, he gives Chelsea a shrug.

"Okay if I borrow a few bucks? I'm gonna stay with her for today, ease her back into the whole thing and get us an Uber back home after."

Chelsea doesn't change her expression, but doesn't break eye contact, either.

"You don't think that might make it harder on her in the long run?"

"It might. But, remember back when we were getting her to sleep in her own room? One of us sleeping next to her all night at first, then sitting in the hall where she could talk to us until she nodded off, then finally she got used to it and we just had to tuck her in?"

"She's not two anymore, though." A moment passes before Chelsea speaks again. "But, I guess she's not twenty, either."

She takes a bill from her pocket bag and hands it to Chris. "Let's try not draw it out, though."

Chris nods, understanding. He's got a new job to look for.

He opens the back door, leans down, and says, "Ready to go back to school. You *and* me?"

Tara's face brightens.

As they walk up to school entrance, Chris glances over his shoulder and gives Chelsea, standing by the driver's door, a look thanking her for putting up with him.

His eyes shift to the two mutants appearing to stand upon the ice not far from the car. He's been aware of the projected beings since seeing them out the windshield while talking to Tara.

He doesn't freak out about seeing them anymore, now that he knows how to patch up his connection to the other world back up whenever it springs a leak. When he gets home, he'll pull out the dollar store notebook he bought a while ago, close his eyes, and put his pen to the lined paper.

He looks away from the mutants and ignores them for now, giving his daughter's hand a good squeeze. She giggles and squeezes back as they walk through the school doors.

ACKNOWLEDGMENTS

Thanks go to Steven Wynne and Russell James for their early feedback and encouragement; to Christoph and Leza for taking in this wild and untamed story and giving it much-needed structure and discipline; and to Don Noble for the cover art.

I'd also like to give a shout out to two novellas—Bryan Smith's THE HALLOWEEN BRIDE and Rick Hautala's COLD RIVER—for showing me it's okay to get crazy and leave logic for later.

And thanks, finally, to Dawn for keeping me around through storm and sunshine.

ABOUT THE AUTHOR

Russell Coy lives with his family in their cat Penelope's house in Northern Indiana. He is also the author of the novelette THE ONE WHO LIES NEXT TO YOU. You can follow him on Twitter at @RussellCoy.

ALSO BY CLASH BOOKS

IN DEFENSE OF SKA

Aaron Carnes

DARRYL

Jackie Ess

NEW VERONIA

M.S. Coe

NIGHTMARES IN ECSTASY

Brendan Vidito

I'M FROM NOWHERE

Lindsay Lerman

HEXIS

Charlene Elsby

WATERFALL GIRLS

Kimberly White

HELENA

Claire Smith

WE PUT THE LIT IN LITERARY

CLASHBOOKS.COM

TWITTER
IG
FB
@clashbooks

Email
clashmediabooks@gmail.com

Publicity
McKenna Rose
clashbookspublicity@gmail.com